Beauty
and the
Beast

STERLING CHILDREN'S BOOKS
New York

TEXT ADAPTATION GIADA FRANCIA • GRAPHIC DESIGN MARINELLA DEBERNARDI

FROM THE FAIRY TALE BY
Jeanne-Marie Leprince de Beaumont

ILLUSTRATIONS BY
Francesca Rossi

In a faraway place
there was a unique city,
which looked like no
other city in the world.

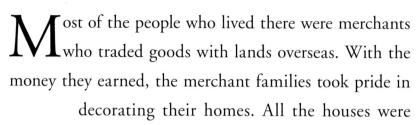

Most of the people who lived there were merchants who traded goods with lands overseas. With the money they earned, the merchant families took pride in decorating their homes. All the houses were embellished with terraces and towers. Humble wooden doors and window frames were replaced with finely sculpted ones. The homes were painted in different colors and so richly decorated that the streets were a delightful patchwork. The city had a unique, cheerful appearance.

Every week, ships left the harbor loaded with all kinds of goods. At sailing time everyone crowded into the main square to bid farewell to the husbands, brothers, and sons, who were going so far away. After many hugs and fond parting words, the women began the long wait for the return of their loved ones. They spent their time spinning, weaving, embroidering, and preparing a happy homecoming.

When the ships returned after many months away, and the cheerful faces of the sailors announced that both the journey and the trading had gone well, everyone went out to meet them with singing and dancing.

The richest and most respected of the merchants was an old gentleman—a widower and the father of three beautiful daughters. The girls were very different from one other. The two eldest were very vain. They had learned to sing, dance, and curtsy gracefully, and to carry on a witty conversation. They had good taste in clothes and jewelry, but that was the extent of their merits.

The youngest was even more beautiful than her sisters. Not only could she dance and sang as well as them, but she had also read hundreds of books. She quietly educated herself in all manner of subjects, enriching her imagination and her thoughts. The girl would even go down to the kitchen, where she learned to cook. In her free time she liked to seek out the children and the old people who were left alone while the men were at sea and provide them with company.

Even when she was small, everyone called her "Belle" because of her bright eyes, beautiful auburn hair, and sweet smile. They continued to do so when she was grown up as well.

Her two older sisters did not appreciate this name. When they heard it, their cheeks would flush red with envy. They would have done anything to be given such a name, and they sought to earn it by dressing themselves up as prettily as they could. Their rooms were always full of clothes, and a jeweler worked for them all the time. They only attended high-society balls and gala evenings at the theater.

Belle, on the other hand, loved the dances organized by the families of the sailors, with whom she danced for whole evenings. Everyone loved her and many young men wanted to marry her. But Belle politely refused each proposal, saying that she felt too young for marriage. Her older sisters, being beautiful and rich too, were also surrounded by suitors. They, however, were arrogant in their refusals.

"We could never stoop to marry merchants like you!" they said. "We will marry only a duke, or an earl at the very least."

One day a letter arrived bearing grave news for the merchant. It was from his friend, a captain, who wrote that the merchant's fleet of ships had been lost at sea. Eager to make ever more money to provide for his daughters, the merchant had invested all his wealth in purchasing rare and valuable goods. The goods were to be brought back from faraway countries by the captains of his ships. The fleet had been due to arrive at the port, but never made it.

The merchant read the letter all the way through, and then looked at his daughters in anguish. He had invested every last cent in the expedition.

The disappearance of the fleet meant the disappearance of everything he owned. There was nothing left. He would have to sell their house and everything in it, and his daughters would have to give up their luxurious clothes and precious jewels. They would all have to move to the country, where the merchant had a small farmhouse.

"My darlings, I am very sorry," said the merchant, with tears in his eyes. "But in the country we will manage to survive, because we have strong arms with which to till the soil. You girls can take care of the vegetable garden and the chicken coop, and, when necessary, the barn and the pig sty. We will also save a lot of money, because we don't need beautiful clothes to work in the fields."

Belle gently patted her father's hand and smiled at him bravely. After all, the country for her meant flowers, birds, clean air, and good health. Her sisters, however, shrieked.

"Never, never will we live in that shack in the middle of nowhere!"

But they too were forced to leave for the country. Their rich suitors had all vanished. The men no longer wanted to know the sisters when the only thing they had left to offer was their nasty personalities.

The family left their beautiful home and their finest possessions in the glorious city, setting out for a new life on the farm.

When they arrived in the country, Belle opened all the windows so that the house was filled with sunshine and birdsong, in the hope that things would seem less sad to her two sisters. But the girls were unmoved. They cried and cried until dinnertime, when they ate a simple meal Belle had prepared with produce from the garden and orchard. Luckily she could cook, and from that day she looked after the kitchen, the barn, the vegetable garden, and the chicken coop. Belle got up at dawn, tidied the house, watered the garden, and took care of the chickens, piglets, and calves. She washed clothes in the stream, and only in her free time did she read a book.

When her tired father returned from the fields, she would prepare a good lunch in a clean and welcoming kitchen. Belle worked all day, singing merrily, and hardly ever seemed tired. Gradually, Belle's cheery outlook gave her father courage. But the two older sisters continued to wail and bemoan the loss of their former life in the city.

Their days were very different from Belle's. Both girls were very lazy, and they preferred to stay in bed until late morning. Then they would go down to breakfast, and afterward walked sadly in the garden doing nothing but complain to each other.

One evening there came a letter. The whole family gathered beside the lamp to read it. The message announced that a ship, laden with goods, had finally arrived in the port. The sisters were unable to hold back their joy.

"We're rich again! At last we can go back to the city," cried the older girl.

"We must get our luggage right away!" said the middle sister. "And when we get home I will be able to buy new clothes and throw away the rags I've been wearing here!"

"Calm down, my dears!" urged the merchant. "It is only one ship. I have to pay the sailors, and I am still in some debt. Wait for my return and then we'll see."

"You're saying these things just to spite us," the older girl said bitterly. "When you come back, bring me a blue velvet dress trimmed with silver lace."

"And for me a pair of satin slippers," added the second.

"I also need an ivory fan, diamond earrings, an emerald necklace, a tiara, and ten lengths of silk to make some new clothes!"

The two girls continued while the merchant listened sadly. Even if he did not have debts to pay, the profit from one ship's cargo would not be enough to buy even half of what the girls wanted. He turned slowly to Belle.

"And do you not want anything, my daughter?" he asked her.

Belle thought. She was content just as she was, but she knew that it would make her father happy to be able to give her a small gift.

"I would like a rose. There are none in the garden. I could plant it, and maybe it would take root."

The merchant smiled, then went straight to bed so that he would wake up early. At dawn the next day he rode out, full of hope. But when he arrived at the port, he discovered that his family would not enjoy any of the riches the vessel had brought home. The sailors had been waiting for months to be paid, and the battered ship had to be repaired from top to bottom. Once he'd paid for everything, the poor man was left with nothing more than a single coin in his pouch.

He got on his horse and galloped out of the city, eager to return to his daughters. But an overturned wagon on the road forced him to take a detour through the forest. The merchant became afraid. He could hear wolves howling, and the wind was so strong that it knocked him from the saddle twice. Just as he began to feel discouraged, he saw a distant light shining through the trees. Taking heart, he urged his horse in that direction.

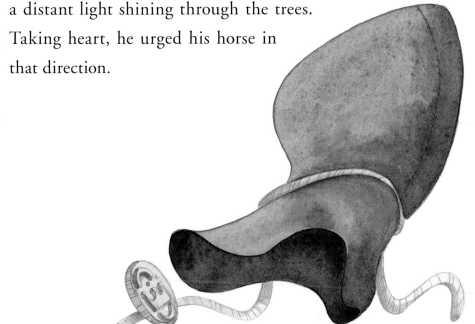

To his surprise, he found himself on the grounds of a beautiful palace.

"What a relief!" he exclaimed. "I'll ask the owners for shelter, so I will not have to spend the night out in the forest."

He tied up his horse and walked toward the palace gates. There were grand courtyards filled with marble statues, but the merchant saw neither servants nor guards. Astonished, he went on until he entered a magnificent garden.

Emerald green lawns, silver streams, flowering plants, and rosebushes all lined a majestic avenue. The merchant strolled down the avenue as if in a dream, then stopped at one of the bushes. Looking at the roses, he remembered Belle and the simple gift she had asked for. So he carefully bent down and took a flower. But at that very moment he heard a terrible cry.

The bushes parted and before him appeared a monstrous creature, part man, part beast.

"Ingrate!" the Beast growled. "I saved your life and you steal my roses, the flowers I cherish most in the world. You must be punished."

"Forgive me," the merchant stammered in terror. "My daughter also loves roses very much, and she asked me to bring her one. I—"

"Enough! I'll grant you your life on one condition: that your daughter comes here in your place. But if she does not come, you must return within three months."

The merchant did not think even for a moment of sending his daughter in his place, but he was relieved that the Beast had left him time to embrace her once more.

As the merchant rode off, he could feel the Beast's eyes upon him.

When at last he returned to the farm, Belle helped him down from his horse. When he saw her, he could not restrain himself and began to cry.

"Father, what has happened?" she asked.

The merchant confessed everything. Belle listened quietly.

"Since the Beast will give you your life in return for mine," she reasoned, "I will take your place and go to the palace."

Despite her father's protests, Belle would have it no other way. She mounted the horse and together they set off for the Beast's palace.

Belle was terrified as they approached the palace, but she knew she was making the right decision. She had asked for that absurd gift, so she felt she was to blame. Nonetheless, her father did not agree.

"I am old, and I have little time left to live. But you, my child, you still have so much to live for!"

"No, Father," Belle said firmly. "If I lost you in this way, I would die of grief, too, because I would feel responsible."

They argued for a long time, and finally decided to enter the palace together. Belle saw the building come into view through the mist and trees. It was gorgeously illuminated, as if awaiting the arrival of a guest. But in the courtyards there was not a living soul.

The horse went alone into the stable, and the time had come for Belle and her father to part. They embraced and wept, then the merchant took his leave. Belle watched him until he disappeared from sight.

Belle's Quarters

Going into the palace, she sought to overcome her despair, thinking, *I have only one more day of life, because surely this evening, the monster will eat me. I want to enjoy this beautiful palace and its wonderful garden.*

The girl roamed through the palace and found surprises at every turn. There were beautiful paintings and precious ornaments in every room. Finally she spotted a plaque fixed to a large door, on which the words "Belle's Quarters" were written. She turned the door handle and gasped at what she saw.

Belle stepped into a gorgeous bedroom. Beyond that were two large rooms, richly furnished with every comfort. The first room was occupied by a grand piano. The second, which was much larger, had been transformed into a library full of books.

Books had always been Belle's best friends, her refuge in times of sadness. She picked one from the shelf, sat down in an armchair, and began to leaf through it. On the title page of the book was written:

Your wish is my command, Belle. In this palace, you are queen.

"There's only one thing I want," whispered the incredulous girl. "To see my father!"

At these words, a large mirror hanging on the wall clouded slightly. Then it cleared, and Belle saw an image in the glass: the kitchen of the little house in the country. In one corner, she saw her two older sisters chatting cheerfully, as if the thought of the rest of the family being in danger had not so much as occurred to them. After a few moments Belle saw her father, undone by grief, sitting sadly by his bed.

When the image faded, she was filled with sadness.

She left the library after several hours of reading and went down to the dining room. There she saw the table was extravagantly laid for two. Uncertain, she sat down in one of the two places and waited. She had just picked up

a glass of water when she heard a loud noise coming from one of the inner rooms. Shortly after, the Beast appeared.

Although she was prepared, Belle felt her heart sink. This creature was truly horrible, even though he spoke quietly and courteously.

"May I sit down and stay here with you while you dine?" the monster asked very politely.

"As you wish," said Belle, "After all, you're the master here."

The Beast shook his head. "No. Here, you are the mistress. If you would prefer not to see me, I will leave immediately."

"Stay, if you like," she responded kindly. "You do not bother me at all."

The monster grinned, but the smile revealed his grotesque fangs. Then he asked, "Do you find me very ugly? Be honest."

Belle trembled, but answered, "Yes. You look ugly. But I think you mean well."

"I try to be good . . . but I'm stupid."

"I don't think so. People who are stupid don't even know it. They never even have this doubt! If you claim to be stupid, it's sure that you're not."

The Beast looked at her with gratitude. "Please eat. And smile, because you're so beautiful when your eyes light up. I would suffer too much if I thought you were unhappy."

"Thank you. You're very kind. Perhaps kinder than any person I've met."

"Then . . . then . . . will you marry me?" stammered the monster.

Belle, who had relaxed and was beginning to enjoy his company, winced at this.

"I will not marry you," she whispered finally, expecting the wrath of the monster.

The beast, however, only sighed, then walked away. Belle watched as he left, and regretted hurting him.

The monster came back the next night, and the girl kept him company for the following three months. It was the most enjoyable and peaceful time that Belle had ever experienced. Together, they enjoyed visiting the huge garden surrounding the palace, dancing to magical music that played on request, and spent countless evenings sitting by the fire reading Belle's favorite books.

One evening, however, the girl approached the Beast with tears in her eyes.

"I saw in the mirror that my father is sick. My sisters are married now, and he is all alone. Please, let me go home to help him."

"What matters most to me is that you are happy," said the Beast. "In the morning you will wake up at home. But do you promise that you will return? If you leave me alone, I will die."

"I will come back, I promise!" replied Belle. "I'll be back in one week."

The Beast looked into her eyes for a long time.

"Take this ring," he said, handing her a gold ring set with a pink sapphire. "When you want to come back, lay it on the table before you go to bed. But remember that I'll be counting the hours. I cannot live without you."

Belle bade him farewell, then went to bed and fell asleep. When she awoke she was astonished to find herself at the small farm in the country, with the chickens clucking below the window.

"Father! Father, I'm back!" she cried, jumping out of bed and running downstairs.

Her father rushed into the house and saw her laughing. Soon they were in each other's arms. He hugged her and kissed her in disbelief.

"I thought you were dead! I missed you! Are you well?"

Belle assured him she was fine and she was happy in the palace with the Beast. At first, her father did not believe her, thinking it was a lie told to console him. But when he saw his daughter's serene smile and glowing eyes, he realized she was truly happy.

"I'm afraid I haven't brought any clothes or supplies," Belle said, freeing herself from her father's embrace. "I didn't bring anything from the palace!"

"At the front door there's a trunk that was not there before, my little one," said her father. "Look! It's full of clothes and jewelry. If you didn't bring it here, who did?"

"It was him!" Belle said with a smile.

When the two older sisters arrived the next day to visit their father, they did not expect to see their younger sister in a new dress fit for a queen. Bursting with envy, they began to complain to each other.

"Why is she so lucky? Why didn't the monster eat her? If he hasn't eaten her yet, he will one day!"

"You're right! We must find a way to set the Beast against her. He loves her too much."

"Let's try to keep her here beyond the week that the Beast allowed," suggested the first sister. "Then the monster will punish her!"

Agreeing, they spent the week lavishing attention and affection on their sister. Belle had never been treated like this and was deeply touched.

"Little sister, stay with us a few more days!" they cried at the end of the week.

Belle hesitated, thinking of the Beast. She did not want to stay away from him. Being away from him made her realize that she missed him. Her father was back to good health, but she could not resist her sisters' pleas. The girl reluctantly promised to stay for another week.

A few days later, Belle had a dream. She saw the Beast consumed with grief, calling her name. He was thin and dragging himself painfully to the edge of a stream at the bottom of the garden. Behind him, the palace windows were dark and the doors were closed. It was a bleak sight. Belle woke up suddenly with her heart pounding.

I was ungrateful, she thought. *I betrayed the trust he showed me.*

Then she was struck with a fear.

"What if it was not just a dream? It seemed so real! What if the Beast is indeed dying because of me?"

As soon as she said these words, Belle was sure that she had been looking at a real scene and not just dreaming it. She looked for the magic ring that would take her back to the castle straight away, not realizing her sisters had secretly taken it. Desperate, she got up, ran to say good-bye to her father, rushed into the barn, and mounted the horse.

Belle arrived at the palace at sunset and began looking high and low for the Beast. She ran up and down the stairs, through one room after another. She called out for him, but heard only her own echo.

The palace was silent and deserted. The place felt horrible without its owner, who, perhaps believing himself forgotten, had died because of her.

At this thought, Belle burst out sobbing. Finally, she came to a halt. She remembered that in her dream she had seen the Beast crawl to the edge of the stream at the bottom of the garden.

"I wonder if . . . " she whispered.

Quick as lightning, she went down the main staircase, and crossed the courtyard into the garden. Right at the bottom, near the stream, she saw the Beast lying under a tree.

"Beast! My dear Beast," Belle screamed.

The girl fell to her knees beside him. She touched his face and then put her hand over his heart. Thankfully, it was still beating. Then Belle ran to the stream, dipped her handkerchief in the cool water, and hurried back to the tree.

Very gently, she lifted the Beast's head and began to bathe his forehead and temples. The Beast's eyes started to open a little. When he saw Belle's beautiful, worried face, he tried to smile.

"Belle, you made me wait so long," he said in a whisper. "I thought you weren't coming back and I didn't want to live anymore. The pain of losing you forever is killing me. But now that I have seen you again I can die happy."

Belle burst into sobs.

"No, dear Beast, don't die! Otherwise I will die too! I could not live without you!" she said through her tears. "How could I go on if you leave me? How will I live? You must get well because I want to marry you, and stay with you forever!"

As soon as she uttered these words, thousands of colorful flashes lit up the sky. Belle looked around, surprised and enchanted by the beauty of the sight, but soon her thoughts returned to her dear Beast. She went to wipe his brow with her wet handkerchief but . . .

The Beast had gone!

Lying under the tree by the brook, there was instead a handsome prince. His perfect features were like those of a statue, but his eyes were full of goodness and affection like those of the Beast. He went down on one knee, took Belle's hand affectionately, and kissed it.

"Where is my dear Beast?" the girl asked, looking around anxiously.

"I am he," said the young man. "I was once a handsome prince, rich and happy, but a jealous witch took everything from me and turned me into the horrible Beast that you knew. I would have stayed that way forever if I had not met a creature capable of loving me in spite of my ugliness. I had lost all hope when you came!"

Hearing his familiar voice and seeing the goodness that sparkled in the eyes of her handsome prince, Belle began to weep again, but this time with joy.

The two young people took each other by the hand. Under a shower of colorful stars made by the fireworks in the sky, they returned to the palace, where they were to be married and live together for many happy years.

STERLING CHILDREN'S BOOKS
New York

An Imprint of Sterling Publishing
387 Park Avenue South
New York, NY 10016

STERLING CHILDREN'S BOOKS and the distinctive Sterling Children's Books
logo are registered trademarks of Sterling Publishing Co., Inc.

First Sterling edition 2015
First published in Italy in 2014 by De Agostini Libri S.p.A.

ISBN 978-1-4549-1507-2

Distributed in Canada by Sterling Publishing
c/o Canadian Manda Group, 165 Dufferin Street
Toronto, Ontario, Canada M6K 3H6
For information about custom editions, special sales,
and premium and corporate purchases,
please contact Sterling Special Sales at 800-805-5489
or specialsales@sterlingpublishing.com.

Translation: Contextus s.r.l., Pavia, Italy (Louise Bostock)
Editor: Contextus s.r.l., Pavia, Italy (Martin Maguire)

Manufactured in China
Lot #:
2 4 6 8 10 9 7 5 3 1
11/14
www.sterlingpublishing.com/kids

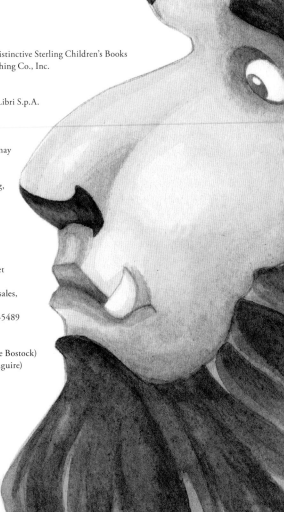